THE PUPPY PLACE

SCRUFFY

THE PUPPY PLACE

Don't miss any of the other stories by Ellen Miles!

THE PUPPY PLACE

SCRUFFY

ELLEN MILES

SCHOLASTIC INC.

For Lauren and the herd

Copyright © 2023 by Ellen Miles
Cover art by Tim O'Brien
Original cover design by Steve Scott

All rights reserved. Published by Scholastic Inc., *Publishers since 1920.* SCHOLASTIC and associated logos are trademarks and/or registered trademarks of Scholastic Inc.

The publisher does not have any control over and does not assume any responsibility for author or third-party websites or their content.

ISBN 978-1-338-84735-2

10 9 8 7 6 5 4 3 2 1   23 24 25 26 27

Printed in the U.S.A.   40
First printing 2023

CHAPTER ONE

"You wouldn't believe what Lizzie did last night," Charles said, panting a little as he tried to keep up with his best friend, Sammy. They were biking home from school on a sunny, warm Friday, the last day of school before spring vacation. Bright green leaves were bursting out all over, and people's yards were full of candy-colored flowers. Charles could smell freshly cut grass and the sweet scent of apple blossoms as they biked under a tree covered in pink-and-white flowers.

"What?" Sammy didn't sound very interested. He pedaled even faster, as if he wanted to get away from Charles.

Charles pedaled harder, too. "She—she told Mom that I was the one who left dirty dishes in the sink. No way! It was her and Maria. Mostly."

"Uh-huh," Sammy said. He stopped pedaling and just coasted as if he wanted to let Charles race on ahead.

"It's just not fair," Charles said, putting on his brakes. "And then when I called her on it, Mom got mad at me, for 'bickering,'" He made a Mom face as he said the word in a Mom voice.

"Uh-huh," Sammy said again.

Charles wished Sammy would say something else. Something like "Wow, that sounds awful. Your sister, Lizzie, really is the worst." After all, Sammy was his best friend. Weren't friends supposed to be supportive and let you know that your feelings mattered? That was what their teacher, Mr. Mason, always said. "It's not fair," Charles repeated. "Don't you think Lizzie is the one who should get in trouble, not me?"

Sammy shrugged. "I guess. Maybe. I don't know."

Charles stopped his bike. "Come on, Sammy. Back me up here!"

Sammy stopped, too. They were right in front of the rickety old gray house they passed every day on the way home from school, the house they sometimes thought might be haunted. Nobody had lived there for years. The front door was boarded up with plywood, the yard was a forest of dead weeds, and the old picket fence around the property had peeling paint and was missing slats.

Charles looked at the house and felt a shiver up his spine. Why had he stopped right at this spot? It was safer to ride past this empty, rickety old place as quickly as he could. But Charles wasn't about to start pedaling again until he knew what Sammy was thinking. He turned his back on the scary house and looked Sammy in the eye. Charles held up his hands in a "well?" gesture.

Sammy frowned. "I don't know," he said. "It's just—I don't get why you and Lizzie have to argue all the time lately. You didn't used to. And neither of you ever argues with the Bean."

The Bean was their little brother. "Who could argue with the Bean?" Charles asked. "All he ever does is laugh and cuddle." He shook his head. "But Lizzie, she's just such a know-it-all, and she gets away with everything. It's like she's my parents' favorite." He looked down at the side-walk and kicked at some weeds that were trying to escape the wild yard by pushing through the spaces in the fence.

"Oh, come on, you know that's not true," said Sammy. "Anyway, if I had a sister I'd never fight with her. It would be like—like fighting with your best teammate. Because that's what you two are, a team. Look at all the puppies you've fostered together! Your family really is a team."

Charles mulled that over. It was true, he and Lizzie usually worked well together when they were taking care of one of the many puppies that the Petersons had fostered, taking care of each one just until they could find it the perfect forever home. "But she always—" he started to argue with Sammy anyway.

"Look," Sammy interrupted. "I don't have any teammates. I'm over here playing all by myself, and believe me, I could use a little backup, too, sometimes."

That made Charles stop and think. He'd always thought Sammy was so lucky to be an only child. Nobody to have to share the last piece of cake with. Nobody to tell you how dumb your ideas are. Nobody to split your parents' love and attention with. Charles had never considered the other part of it. The lonely part.

But he put his hands on his hips and grinned at Sammy. "Oh, believe me, you'd fight sometimes," Charles said. "Sisters are soooo annoying."

"Maybe," said Sammy. "But anyway, hearing about your arguments with Lizzie is kind of boring."

"That's what Dad says!" Charles said. "He says, 'How can you stand all that bickering over nothing? It's so boring!'" Charles sighed. It wasn't like he *wanted* to argue all the time. But he had to stand up for himself, didn't he? "It's just—"

He stopped and listened for a moment.

He gulped.

"Wait. What's that noise?" he whispered.

Sammy cocked his head, and his eyes went

wide. Charles could tell that he'd heard it, too. An eerie, high-pitched wailing.

Charles glanced at the falling-down house and felt that shiver down his back again. He straightened up his bike and put his foot on a pedal. "Let's get out of here," he said.

"Wait," said Sammy. "I don't think it's coming from the house." He cupped his ear and listened. "It's coming from over there," he said, pointing to an overgrown bush that almost hid part of the broken-down fence. He started to walk toward it, slowly and quietly.

Charles felt frozen in place. What was Sammy doing? The last place Charles wanted to be was anywhere closer to that spine-tingling sound. He watched as Sammy got closer to the wild bush, then bent down and pushed aside a tangle of branches. *"Stop!"* Charles wanted to yell. This was like a scary movie. What if something even scarier happened, like a hand reaching out to grab Sammy?

But Sammy just pushed in even farther. Then he pushed back out, fast. "Charles!" he called in a low voice. He waved an arm. "You have to come here and see this."

"Um," Charles said. He still felt like he couldn't move.

"Charles!" hissed Sammy. "Come on! Now!"

Charles got off his bike and took a few steps, feeling as if he was walking through quicksand. *Wishing* he was walking through quicksand. That would be better than walking up to a ghost. "What—what is it?" he asked as he came closer to Sammy, who had pushed all the branches away from the fence.

"It's a puppy," said Sammy.

CHAPTER TWO

Meanwhile, a few blocks away, Charles's sister, Lizzie, walked along the sidewalk with her best friend, Maria. Lizzie held three dogs on three different leashes: Franklin, a friendly corgi; a twinkle-pawed mini poodle named Gigi; and a solidly built German shepherd who was, naturally, named Tank. Maria was walking two other dogs: a long-eared hound mix named Gomer and a sassy little Yorkie named Biggie. Lizzie and Maria had a dog-walking business, along with two other friends, and spent most weekday afternoons taking care of their clients. Sometimes they each did their route alone; other times, like today, Lizzie and Maria decided to walk together.

"Really, you wouldn't believe how annoying Charles is being lately," Lizzie was saying. "He never does his chores when he's supposed to, he constantly tells the most unfunny jokes you've ever heard, and Mom and Dad always take his side—"

Maria stopped walking, tightening her hold on her leashes so the dogs wouldn't surge ahead. She held up her hand. "Really, Lizzie? I'm so tired of hearing you complain about Charles. What happened to you two? You used to get along so well. It always made me want a little brother, just to see the way he looked up to you and how you watched out for him."

Lizzie stooped to check Tank's collar. It seemed a little loose. Was he losing weight? She ran a hand over his ribs. No, he was just right. "I don't know," she said. "I kind of miss those days, to be honest. And I know Mom and Dad sure do. They are really sick of hearing us argue all the time. They even said we aren't going to be allowed to foster anymore if we keep it up."

Lizzie bit her lip. They couldn't really mean that, could they? Fostering was the best thing in the world. The Petersons had gotten to know—and cuddle, and play with—so many amazing puppies. Some of the puppies had been challenging, but the only really tough part was how hard it was to give them up when the time came. They hadn't been able to part with one of their fosters, Buddy. He was now part of the family. Lizzie smiled as she thought of her sweet brown pup with the heart-shaped white spot on his chest.

"Hey," said Maria. "Isn't that Charles right now?"

"What? Where?" Lizzie straightened up and

peered down the street. Somebody was riding toward them on a bicycle—fast! Yes, that yellow helmet with the flame decals, that was Charles's.

He raced straight for them, slamming on the brakes at the last moment. Tank stepped between Lizzie and the bicycle as if to protect her; that was just the kind of dog he was. "It's okay, Tank," she said, giving his back a calming stroke. "Charles! What's up?" Her brother looked upset.

"Puppy," Charles said, panting hard as he leaned on his handlebars. "Stuck. Needs help. Came for you."

Lizzie looked at Maria, eyebrows raised. "A puppy?" she asked, looking back at Charles. "Where?"

Charles took a deep breath. Maria put out a hand, patting his shoulder. "It's okay, Charles. Take a moment."

But Lizzie was impatient. "Charles! Where's the puppy?"

"By the scary house," he said. "On the way home from school. You know, the one with the broken-down fence in front? The gray one?" He took another deep breath.

Lizzie nodded. "Sure," she said. "But where's the puppy, exactly?" She was already figuring out how quickly she could drop off the dogs she was walking. "And what do you mean about the puppy being stuck? What kind of puppy is it? Is it hurt?"

Charles looked back at her, wide-eyed. He didn't seem able to speak at first, but then he stammered out some details. "He's a little puppy, all kind of scraggly like he's been by himself for a while. He's stuck, like his head is stuck between two slats in that old wooden fence." He gulped. "When you come up close to him he shows all his teeth—I didn't hear him growling or anything, but it was still kind of scary." He stopped, catching his breath. "Sammy's there with him, just trying to keep him calm. But—how are we going to get him out?"

"Charles," Maria said gently. "Do you think we need a grown-up to help?"

Charles nodded. "I think so," he said. "Yes, definitely."

"Okay." Lizzie shot Maria a grateful look, then turned back to Charles. "You ride home and get Dad. I'll meet you at the scary house. Don't worry, we'll help the puppy."

Charles nodded again, but he didn't move.

"Go!" said Lizzie. "But—ride carefully. Watch out for cars. Okay?"

"Okay," said Charles. He turned his bike around, put a foot on a pedal, and took off.

Lizzie looked at Maria, a question in her eyes.

"Of course," said Maria, reading her friend's mind. She reached out and took the three leashes Lizzie handed her. "I'll finish your route and get them all home safe. You go check on this puppy."

Lizzie took a deep breath as she watched Charles ride around the corner. He loved dogs as much as she did, and she could tell that he was very upset about finding this stuck puppy. She was glad to know that he'd be home in a minute, where Dad would be ready to listen and help. Dad was always ready to listen and help—that's why he was so good at his job as a firefighter and EMT.

"Thanks, Maria," Lizzie said as she headed off toward the old gray house, just a few blocks away.

"Sammy!" she called as she came around the corner. She waved to him and he waved back. When she got closer, she saw that Charles's friend was sitting on the sidewalk, close to the puppy but not close enough to get bitten. That was good.

"I'm just talking to him," he said in a low voice when Lizzie sat down next to him.

Lizzie nodded. "That's great," she said. She looked at the puppy, or at least at his head, the only part she could see from this side of the fence. "Some kind of terrier mix," she murmured, noticing the longish, coarse tan coat and the wild eyebrows framing bright eyes. Lizzie prided herself on having practically memorized the "Dog Breeds of the World" poster on her bedroom wall. Very slowly, she put out a hand for him to sniff. "Hi, pup," she whispered.

The puppy bared his teeth as he ducked his head, looking up at Lizzie. The whites of his eyes were showing beneath those bushy eyebrows.

I—I don't know! I'm a little scared. You're so big and I'm so tiny!

"Oh!" said Lizzie, pulling her hand back. "It's okay, little one. We're not going to hurt you." She turned to Sammy. "I don't think he's snarling," she said. "I think that's a smile. Dogs do that sometimes when they want to show that they're not a threat. He's trying to let us know that he won't hurt us."

"Um, okay," said Sammy. "If you say so. But I'm still not going to pet him."

"Good idea," said Lizzie. "We don't know anything for sure, yet." She peered down the street. "Here comes Charles—with our dad." She felt relief wash over her when she saw her father walking toward them, his long stride forcing Charles to trot in order to keep up. This little pup was in trouble, and now they were going to be able to help him.

CHAPTER THREE

Charles started to run as soon as he saw his sister squatting by the puppy. Dad's medical backpack bumped against Charles's legs: He was carrying it since Dad's hands were full. In one hand Dad held his toolbox, and in the other he carried a puppy crate, a safe place to put the puppy if they got him free. Charles was really glad Lizzie was there. She was probably already making the puppy feel better. She was great that way; it was like she knew how to speak Dog. "Is he okay?" he called as he got closer.

"He's just scared," Lizzie said, putting her

finger to her lips as she gave Charles the signal to quiet down.

"I know, I know," Charles said under his breath. Why did Lizzie have to be so bossy? Obviously he wasn't about to go yelling into the puppy's ears. He knew how to act around dogs, too. Lizzie wasn't the only one. He started to say more, but his friend interrupted.

"Charles," Sammy said, giving him a look.

Charles knew that look meant *Don't start fighting with Lizzie*. He knew Sammy was right. The important thing was the puppy. Charles squatted down a safe distance from the puppy's head. "Poor thing," he said. "I bet he's ready to get out of there."

"And I don't think it'll take long," said Dad, from behind Charles. "This old fence is so rickety. I'll be able to take out a couple of slats just using my hammer." He put down the toolbox and opened it up. He glanced at the old house. "I would ask the owners first, but I don't think anyone's lived here for years."

"Just don't scare the puppy," Lizzie said. "No sudden moves. We can set up the crate in front of the fence so he'll walk right into it when he's freed."

Charles rolled his eyes. Lizzie was so bossy and always had to act like her ideas were the best. "Maybe Sammy and I should go around to the other side of the fence," he suggested. "That way he won't try to turn around and run off."

"Great idea," Dad said.

Charles beamed—and grinned even wider when he caught Lizzie rolling her eyes.

"Just don't get too close to him," Dad said.

"We won't," said Charles as he opened the creaky gate and pushed his way into the overgrown yard, Sammy following behind. Charles didn't give the abandoned house a second thought. Even if there were ghosts in there, he didn't care. He just wanted to help the puppy. He was sure that Sammy felt the same.

"Awww!" they both said as they came around the corner and saw the back end of the puppy. He had short little legs, scruffy fur that looked like it had been gelled and spiked, and a sort of scrawny but adorable tail. And the tail was wagging, double-time!

I know you want to help me. I can just tell! Please get me out of here and I'll be your friend forever.

Charles was glad to see that scraggly little tail wagging. That meant that the puppy probably wasn't angry or even too scared. It was as if he knew they were there to help him.

"Okay," said Lizzie. "I've got the puppy crate

in place." She'd moved it to right in front of the puppy.

"Good," said Dad. He reached out to wiggle one of the slats that was trapping the puppy. "Really loose," he said. He bent down and pulled a hammer out of his toolbox. "Ready?" he asked. "Just knocking this one out might do it."

"Ready," said Charles and Sammy together.

"Ready," said Lizzie.

Dad tapped on the top end of the wooden slat, and right away it began to fall inward, toward Charles and Sammy. The puppy stopped wagging his tail, and Charles saw him take two steps backward.

What was that noise? What's going on? What— hey! I'm free!

"Oh no, you don't," Charles said, taking a step forward. Next to him, Sammy did the same.

The puppy reversed direction, pushing through the hole in the fence toward the sidewalk, and popped right into the puppy crate.

Lizzie snaked out a hand to close and latch the door. "Gotcha!" she cried.

Charles wanted to give her a "shhh!" finger to the lips, but he was too happy to bother with that. "Yay!" he said. "A new foster puppy! Let's take him right home." He was so excited to get to know this scruffy little guy.

But Dad seemed to have other ideas. "Hold on, there," he said, holding up a hand.

Charles and Lizzie exchanged a glance. They were both used to this. Mom and Dad always seemed to have the ridiculous idea that they had to think things over before they took on a new foster puppy.

"But Dad," Charles said. "We have to foster him! He needs us!"

"He won't be any trouble," Lizzie said. "He's just a little dude."

Both of them were wearing their best "Plllleeeeeeeasssssse?" faces, just like Buddy's when he wanted a lick of your ice cream.

Dad shook his head, laughing. "I didn't say we couldn't foster him. I think that would be great! But I also think that the first thing this puppy needs is a visit to Dr. Gibson."

"Oh," Charles said.

"Right," Lizzie said.

They both let their faces go back to normal.

Dr. Gibson was their vet, and she was great about looking over their new foster puppies in case they needed any medical attention. She was the best. Plus, she would scan the puppy for an ID chip, in case he belonged to someone who was looking for him. Which Charles doubted. He squatted down to take a look inside the puppy crate. This guy hadn't had a bath or a good meal in a long time, Charles was pretty sure about that. But he was in good hands now. This little puppy was going to be taken care of.

CHAPTER FOUR

"We'll head home and get the van," Dad said. "We can grab a snack and call Dr. Gibson, and hopefully drive the puppy right over to see her." He reached down to pick up a handle on one side of the puppy crate. "Help me out, Lizzie," he said.

Lizzie loved being Dad's helper for anything: handing him his screwdriver when he was fixing something, finding his slippers, chopping vegetables when he cooked. Helping with a puppy was best of all. She grabbed the handle on the other side and she and Dad started off down the sidewalk.

"You boys can bring the other things," he called

over his shoulder. Sammy picked up the toolbox. Charles didn't budge. He just stood there, frowning, arms crossed against his chest.

"It's not fair," Lizzie heard him mumble. Then he spoke louder. "Why does she always get to be your helper?"

Lizzie looked up at Dad, just in time to see him sigh, his shoulders sagging. "You can take turns, okay?" he said. "Just grab my medical bag for now. We want to get this guy to the vet, don't we?"

Grumbling, Charles picked up the backpack and followed the others. He counted the houses they passed, and after a block and a half he stopped, clearing his throat loudly. Lizzie looked back at her brother. "My turn," he said. "Tradesies." He pointed to the medical bag.

"Really?" Lizzie asked. "We're almost home."

"Exactly," said Charles. "That's why it's my turn." Why did he have to explain everything?

Lizzie heard Dad sigh. "I think you two can handle it from here," he said, waving Charles up to take his side of the crate. "It's not heavy at all, even with the puppy inside."

"But then she gets to carry the puppy the whole way!" Charles said. "It's not fair!"

Now Lizzie saw Sammy heave a big sigh. "Gotta go," he said, handing the toolbox to Dad before taking off down the sidewalk.

When they got home, Charles and Lizzie bickered over whether to let the puppy out of the crate. They argued over which of them got to call Dr. Gibson's office. When they got into the van for the trip to the vet's, they squabbled over who got the window seat.

"If you two can't keep it together while we're here," Dad said as he pulled up in front of the vet's office, "I'm going to call Mom and ask her to pick you both up while the puppy gets examined.

I know Dr. Gibson would not want to hear the two of you go on like this. Nobody does."

Lizzie made the "zipping my lip" gesture.

"Okay, Dad," Charles said as he climbed out of the van. Honestly, he was tired of their fighting, too. But why should he let Lizzie get her way all the time just because she was older?

"Well, hello there!" said Lila, the receptionist, as they walked into the vet's office. She peered into the crate that Dad had lifted onto the counter, taking a closer look. "Check you out, smiley!" She laughed. "What a character!" Lila waved them through. "Dr. Gibson will be right with you," she said.

The vet tech met them in the examination room. "Hi, I'm Rachel," she said. "You can take the puppy out now if you like." She busied herself with wiping down a counter, seeming too shy to make chitchat.

Dad opened the door of the crate and lifted the puppy out onto the exam table.

"Ohhh," said Rachel. Her eyes lit up when she saw the scruffy little pup.

"Awwww," Charles and Lizzie said together. This was their first really good look at the puppy they'd helped rescue. He was such a little guy, with that brownish spiky hair and scrawny tail. Even his ears were crooked, one up and one down. He pulled back his lips as they all looked at him, showing a mouthful of scraggly teeth. He was not the type of perfectly groomed dog you'd see in the arms of a celebrity on the cover of a magazine— but Charles thought he was adorable in his own way. He could tell Lizzie did, too; her eyes shone as she gazed at his funny little face.

Dr. Gibson liked him, too. "What a great grin you have," the vet said to the puppy as she came into the room. She began to run her hands over his sides, moving slowly so as not to scare him. She hummed and murmured to the puppy as she examined him, and he seemed to relax at her touch. "Nice to meet you, Scruffy," she said, smiling back at him.

The vet loved to make up nicknames on the spot for their foster puppies. She usually picked perfectly, like when she had first met another of their fosters who needed lots of medical help but whose spirit was always upbeat. She had named that puppy Sparky.

"How can you tell that he's grinning, not snarling?" Charles asked.

"Experience, mainly," said the vet. "I'm just used to seeing the difference between a smile and a snarl. *But*"—she raised a warning finger—"you should know that some dogs smile because they are afraid. And sometimes a frightened dog will bite. So don't ever assume that the smile means that a dog is happy or friendly."

She ruffled Scruffy's fur. "In this case, I think she's very friendly. Just maybe quite shy and out of practice with how to get along with humans."

"Wait, did you just say 'she'?" Charles asked.

Dr. Gibson smiled. "That's right," she said. "Surprise! Scruffy's definitely a girl."

Charles and Lizzie stared at each other, then back at Scruffy. "A girl!" said Lizzie. "Cool!"

"Do you think she's okay?" Charles asked. "I mean, she's not hurt or anything, right?" He reached out slowly to give Scruffy a gentle pat, now that Dr. Gibson had said she was friendly. The puppy ducked her head and smiled at him, showing a whole mouthful of teeth. Her ears twitched and her scrawny tail wagged back and forth as if she wasn't quite sure that he was a friend.

Oh, hi! Really? You like me? That makes me happy.

"Well, I'd say she's been living rough for quite a while," said Dr. Gibson. "Maybe even her whole life. She's probably only about six to eight months old now." She ran her hands over Scruffy's ribs. "She's skinny and obviously hasn't been bathed or groomed for a long time, if ever. And there's no microchip or collar, so I'm guessing she's been a stray for some time."

"But she's basically healthy?" Lizzie asked. "Great! So, we can take her home with us?"

"Yes—and no," said Dr. Gibson. "She does seem surprisingly healthy, considering her hard life— but you can't take her home just yet. I'm going to want to board her overnight to keep an eye on her. We'll make sure she has all her shots, give her some fluids and some food, and tuck her into a comfy place to get a good sleep."

Rachel, the vet tech, must have seen Charles's and Lizzie's faces fall.

"I can sleep on the cot in the kennel room," she said. She had been snapping photos of Scruffy with her phone while Dr. Gibson examined the pup. "So she won't be alone. And I can send you photo updates tonight and tomorrow morning." She ducked her head and smiled. "To be honest, I'm kinda shy, too—so I think Scruffy and I will get along great."

Lizzie and Charles thanked her, said good-bye to Scruffy and Dr. Gibson, and followed Dad out to the van. It was great that Scruffy was healthy, but it was so hard to leave without her. They climbed in silently, too bummed to even fight over the window seat.

CHAPTER FIVE

Later, at dinnertime, Charles poked at a couple of peas on his plate. "May I be excused?" he asked. He didn't feel hungry at all.

"Three more peas," said Mom.

"Four," said Dad.

Charles speared exactly four peas and ate them up. Then he pushed back his chair.

"Lizzie, it looks like you're finished eating, too. You're also excused," Dad said. "In fact, I'd like the two of you to go up to your rooms and do a little bit of thinking about how you're going to start getting along. Then we're going to have a family conference."

Dinner that night had been a quiet meal. Charles knew that Mom and Dad were both annoyed that he and Lizzie had squabbled over whose turn it was to set the table. But it was hard to be nice when he felt so disappointed about leaving Scruffy at the vet's. It wasn't like that was Lizzie's fault or anything, but still.

Charles plodded upstairs, followed by Lizzie. He went into his room, closed the door, and flopped down on his bed. Then he jumped up. He needed Buddy to cuddle with. He went out into the hall and called for the little brown puppy. "Buddy! Where are you?"

"He's in here," he heard Lizzie call from her room.

Well, that wasn't fair. Buddy wasn't supposed to be Lizzie's dog. He was the whole family's dog, but Lizzie always hogged him. "Dad!" Charles called down the stairs. "Lizzie won't—"

"I don't want to hear it," Dad called back before Charles could even finish. Charles stood at the top of the stairs for a moment, then went back to his room. He lay down and hugged his pillow, pretending it was Buddy. Or Scruffy. Or any sweet, warm puppy.

A little while later, he heard the Bean laughing in the bathtub as Dad gave him a bath, then giggling in his bed when Mom read him a story, doing all the funny voices. Sometimes Charles missed being the Bean's age.

Soon after, there was a knock on his door. "Come on downstairs, Charles," Mom said. Then he heard her knock on Lizzie's door.

Downstairs, Dad sat on the couch. "Come sit by me," he said to Charles, patting the couch. Then he had Lizzie sit on his other side. "Listen, you two," he said. "I know it's not always easy to get along, but you used to do really well at it. I don't know why you've gotten into this habit of arguing, but it really has to stop."

"Fine, as long as he—" Lizzie began. Dad put a finger to his lips and shook his head.

"No buts," he said.

"I can be nice," said Charles, "but I don't know about—"

Mom shook her head at him, holding up a hand as if to say "Stop right there." "If we're going to foster this puppy I'm hearing about," she said, "you two are going to have to work together to take care of her. I'm in the middle of a big article and Dad's squad is helping to build a new gazebo downtown. We're both very busy."

Mom was a newspaper reporter for the *Littleton News*, and Charles knew that a deadline meant she would be working hard. "We always help with the puppies," Charles said.

"Yes, that's true. But this time you'll need to do more than just help," said Mom. "Between the two of you, you're going to have to be a hundred percent responsible for this puppy. It's a good thing that you don't have school this week, so you'll have plenty of time."

"That means walking him—I mean, her—when she needs a walk, and feeding her on time," Dad said. "And making sure that she and Buddy are getting along, and—"

"We can do it," Lizzie interrupted him. "Actually, I could do it by myself."

Charles raised his eyebrows. "Oh, really?" he asked.

Mom held up a hand again. "You're going to have to pull together as a team," she said. "If you keep arguing, it's just not going to work. And if we feel like it's not working"—she exchanged a look with Dad—"the puppy will have to go to Caring Paws."

That was the animal shelter where Lizzie volunteered sometimes. It was a terrific place, and Ms. Dobbins, the director, was really nice. But Charles hated to think of a little stray like Scruffy having to spend her days and nights in a kennel if she could be in their comfy house with Buddy for company.

"Look," said Dad. "We love you both so much, and we know how much you love each other. Your mom and I are hoping you can take this opportunity to remind yourselves what a great team you can be when you're working together."

"Sure, you love us both," Charles said under his breath. "But Lizzie more."

"What?" Mom asked. "Listen, you." She pulled him onto her lap. "We love you and Lizzie and the Bean so much that our hearts are bursting. I couldn't possibly love you—or Lizzie, or the Bean—more than I do. I love you each in different ways, for different reasons, because you are different people. But you're all my very favorite people in the world."

"Ditto," said Dad, pulling Lizzie onto his lap. She squirmed a bit—she liked to pretend she was too old for laps—but then she put her arms around his neck.

For a second, Charles felt jealous—until he remembered he was in Mom's lap, and he remembered what she had said. "We can do it," he said. "Right, Lizzie? We can get along."

"Definitely," said Lizzie, her voice muffled by Dad's shoulder. She held out a pinky for a pinky shake. "Buds?" she asked.

Charles linked his pinky in hers. "Best buds a-oo-gah!" he chanted.

Lizzie laughed. "Best buds, a-oo-gah," she chanted back.

Then they did it once together, shaking their

linked pinkies up and down for emphasis. "Best buds, a—ooooo—gah!"

Mom and Dad sort of laughed and groaned at the same time. The whole "best buds" chant had started last summer during a long road trip, and Mom and Dad had definitely gotten tired of hearing it. But Charles could tell, by the way they were smiling at each other, that it sounded pretty good to them now.

"So, when can we pick up Scruffy?" he asked.

CHAPTER SIX

"Oh, look at her!" Lizzie clasped her hands in front of her chest, gazing at Scruffy. "She looks, like, a million times better!"

Lizzie and Charles and Mom were at Dr. Gibson's the next morning, picking up their new foster puppy.

"She's feeling better, too," said Dr. Gibson. "Definitely ready to check out her new foster home."

"I even gave her a bath this morning," said Rachel.

"Wow, she really is adorable," Mom said, nodding.

Lizzie was glad Mom hadn't seen the "before"

version of Scruffy. This "after" version was much better. Her fur was soft and silky looking and her eyes were bright. She stood on her hind legs and wagged her tail—still scrawny but much cleaner—seeming happy to see them. She ducked her head and smiled her snaggletoothed smile, giving Lizzie a shy glance.

You're the ones who saved me! Thank you, thank you, thank you!

Everyone burst out laughing as Rachel held up her phone, trying to capture the moment. "She's the cutest," she said, agreeing with Mom. "And she already has seventeen followers."

"Oh?" Mom raised her eyebrows.

Rachel laughed. "I made Scruffy her own account, just for fun. I don't really do social media, but I couldn't resist. My friends are all in love with her smile. Send me pictures and I'll keep posting!"

Dr. Gibson shrugged and raised her hands in a "what can you do?" motion. "I don't think I'd have the first idea of how to get seventeen followers, whatever that even means," she said. "But obviously Scruffy does." She petted the little dog, then picked her up off the exam table and set her down on the floor, holding out the leash to Charles and Lizzie. "She's all yours," she said. "I'm sure you'll find her a wonderful home."

Lizzie reached for the leash—of course, as the oldest and most knowledgeable about dogs, she should be the one in charge—but then she pulled her hand back. Why not let Charles enjoy the moment? She waved him forward—and after a quick *really?* look, he took the leash. Lizzie glanced at Mom and saw her nod and smile. Good. It wasn't so hard to get along with Charles, really.

At home, Charles and Lizzie took Scruffy straight out to the backyard so the new puppy could explore. Once Scruffy had a chance to get a feel for her new home, they let Buddy out: This was their usual routine when they brought home a foster pup. As always, Buddy made friends right away. Soon he and Scruffy were dashing around the yard, playing keep-away with Buddy's squeaky football.

"She fits right in," said Charles, watching them.

Lizzie heard a certain wistful tone in his voice. "You're wishing we could keep her, aren't you?" she asked. She put a hand on his shoulder. "Me, too."

Lizzie almost always wished they could keep their foster puppies. She fell in love with them all. Plus, she knew how much Buddy would love having a sibling. But that wasn't how fostering worked, and Mom and Dad had made it clear that one permanent dog was enough if they were going to continue to be a foster family.

Lizzie and Charles got along well all that day. Together, they took Scruffy on a walk around the neighborhood. Together, they started to teach her some basic manners, like how to sit and stay. By evening time they still hadn't squabbled all day, and they set the table for dinner together, too—even though Lizzie was sure it was actually Charles's turn.

At dinner, they chatted about their day with Scruffy. And when they were finished, they both jumped up to clear away everyone's dishes.

When Lizzie came back to the table to pick up the last of the glasses, Mom smiled at her. "I knew you two could get along if you tried," she said. "How about a movie night as soon as we get the Bean to bed?"

"Sounds great," said Lizzie, smiling back. She

had to admit that it was nice to get along with Charles. She definitely did not miss the knot in her stomach or the yucky feelings she always had after they argued.

Lizzie and Charles picked out a movie together, again without any squabbling, and settled in on the couch with Buddy and Scruffy, waiting for Mom and Dad to come down and join them.

But Scruffy couldn't seem to get settled. She pawed at Charles's leg, then jumped up and trotted across the living room, heading toward the kitchen. She looked back, smiling at them. Then she trotted back to Lizzie and put a paw on her knee, smiling some more as she let out a little whine.

There's something I want. Something I need! Can't you understand?

She was doing this for the third time when

Mom came downstairs. "What's the matter with Scruffy?" she asked.

"No idea," said Lizzie. "Maybe she's just having a hard time getting used to our house."

Mom shook her head. "I don't think so," she said. "I think she's hungry. Which one of you gave her dinner?"

"Charles did," said Lizzie.

"Lizzie did," said Charles at the exact same time.

They stared at each other. "I thought you were going to feed her," said Charles.

"I said I'd do it every *other* day," said Lizzie. Obviously, that meant she would start tomorrow. "So it was your turn."

"No way!" Charles said. "You're just saying that now because you totally forgot!"

"What?" Lizzie couldn't believe her ears. "You—"

"Hey!" Mom clapped her hands.

Lizzie and Charles stopped arguing and looked up at her. "Your foster puppy is hungry," Mom said. "And you arguing about it is not helping to get food into her bowl." She shook her head. "You were doing so well," she muttered as she left the room and headed back upstairs.

Movie night was canceled. Hopefully, their time with Scruffy was not. Lizzie jumped up to feed the puppy, feeling that knot in her stomach all over again. When she came back to the couch, she looked very serious. "We have to fix this," she said to Charles.

"I know," Charles said. "We can't lose Scruffy. She needs us. But how do we stop arguing?"

Just let me be in charge, Lizzie thought. But out loud, she said, "Maybe we should make a sched-ule for all the puppy chores. Like, at least that would show Mom and Dad that we're trying to do things right."

Charles raised his eyebrows. "That's actually a pretty good idea," he said slowly.

Lizzie could tell that he hated to admit it, but of course he had to. It *was* a good idea. She always had good ideas—why couldn't everyone else see that? She jumped up to get some paper and markers. Once again, she was going to fix things. What would their foster puppies do without her?

CHAPTER SEVEN

"We're really sorry," Charles said to both parents at breakfast the next morning.

"We made a schedule," Lizzie added quickly, showing them the calendar that she and Charles had worked on the night before. "See, it shows whose turn it is to feed Scruffy or to take her out for walks."

Dad nodded. "Well done," he said, looking it over.

"But remember," Mom said, "a schedule is only good if you follow it." Her gaze moved to the Chore Chart posted on the fridge—the one that Lizzie and Charles somehow never remembered to check.

"We will," Charles said. "We promise." He looked down at Scruffy, who sat next to the Bean's chair, watching carefully for any dropped bits of food. At the same moment, she looked up at him and smiled her goofy smile. She tilted her head and wagged her tail.

Hey, you can't blame me for hoping for scraps, can you? I've been living on my own for a long time.

Charles laughed. Scruffy was shy, but she was also a sassy little thing. That head tilt! She was so cute. "Lizzie's volunteering at Caring Paws this morning so I'm going to take Scruffy for a walk around the neighborhood," he said. "Sammy's coming with me."

Dad nodded approvingly. "Very good," he said. "I'm glad you two are working together."

"And I gave her breakfast," Lizzie added.

"Great," said Mom.

Charles grinned at Lizzie, and she gave him a thumbs-up. Nobody was sending Scruffy away quite yet. They had been given another chance to show that they could cooperate.

After breakfast, Charles let both dogs out into the backyard to run around for a while. Then he clipped a leash onto Scruffy's collar. "Want to explore your new neighborhood?" he asked her. They headed off, and Sammy ran out to join them as they passed his house, next door.

"Smile, Scruffy!" Sammy said. He cracked up when she tilted her head at him and showed all her teeth. "That is hilarious," he said. "She should be on TV or something."

They walked on until a teenage boy stopped them on the corner. "Hey, isn't that Scruffy? She looks just like that dog on the Internet." He bent down to say hi. "Can I get a smile?" he asked. Of course, Scruffy gave him a grin.

A mom with two toddlers was the next to recognize her. "Scruffy!" she cried. "I'm one of your biggest fans!" Scruffy smiled at her, too. "Awww! She really does smile, doesn't she? Can I get a selfie with her?" The mom knelt down and took a picture with her phone, squeezing herself, her two kids, and Scruffy into the shot.

"Wow," said Sammy as they walked along. "I guess Scruffy doesn't have to be on TV. She's famous already."

"Charles!" called someone from behind them just then. It was Rachel, the vet tech from Dr. Gibson's. "Hey," she said, catching up to them. "Your mom said I'd probably find you out this way." She bent down to pet Scruffy and giggled when the puppy smiled at her. "Guess what," she said.

"Scruffy's gone viral?" Sammy asked.

Charles knew that meant that something had really taken off on the Internet, so that basically everyone knew about it. That would explain why strangers were stopping them on the street.

Rachel looked surprised. "Um, yes. She sort of has."

"I thought only your friends knew about her," Charles said.

"And their friends, and friends of those friends, and"—Rachel shrugged, holding up her hands—"I know, it's wild." She held up her phone to show Charles and Sammy. "See? She has nine thousand likes on her last post. Everybody loves Scruffy. I need more pictures to post. That's why I came over." She bent down to pick Scruffy up. "And to see you, of course," she said, nuzzling the puppy's neck.

Rachel walked with Sammy and Charles for a

while, snapping photos of everything Scruffy did, from peeing on a clump of dandelions to sniffing a mailbox. And of course she snapped away whenever Scruffy smiled. People kept stopping them to say hello and ask for selfies. Rachel was shy with them at first, but after the third time she was chatting away, telling about how Scruffy got her name and about what her smiles probably meant. "My boss, Dr. Gibson, says that by now it's more of a learned behavior," she told one woman. "She gets positive attention when she smiles, so she does it more and more." She grinned down at Scruffy. "Isn't that right, Scruffy McScruffy-face?"

Scruffy gazed back up at her, grinning and wagging her tail.

Whatever you're saying, you're right. I love the sound of your voice.

At suppertime that night, Charles told everyone about Scruffy's fame. "We won't have any trouble finding her a home," he said. "Everybody loves Scruffy."

"But it has to be the *right* home," Lizzie said.

"Of course!" said Charles, smiling at his sister. They'd been getting along all day, and that made him happy.

After dinner, Charles settled in on the couch with the book he'd been reading. He couldn't wait to see how it turned out. Buddy lay next to him, and Charles stroked his silky ears. "You know I'll always love you best," he whispered to the little brown pup. Sometimes Buddy needed a little extra attention when they had a foster pup in the house.

A little while later, Charles heard a whimpering sound. "Lizzie, can you let Scruffy out?" he called. Lizzie was doing a craft at the kitchen table.

"Today's your day for walking her," Lizzie called back. "I'm in the middle of something."

"Oh, come on," called Charles. "I don't want to make Buddy get up."

"You mean *you* don't want to get up," Lizzie said.

Just then Mom swooped through the living room. A second later Charles heard the sliding doors to the back deck open. *Uh-oh*, he thought. He set Buddy down on the floor and got up to see what was happening. Lizzie got up, too.

A few moments later, Mom came back inside with Scruffy. "Come here, you two," she said. When Lizzie and Charles joined her, she pointed at the scruffy little pup. "This poor little puppy almost just peed on the floor, right here by the door," she said, "while you two were arguing about who should take her out. She was doing her best—she really wanted to get out there—but nobody was listening to her." Mom shook her head. "I know you two are trying, but you're just not holding up your end of the deal. We're going to have to call Ms. Dobbins in the morning."

She headed upstairs without saying another word.

"Wow," said Charles.

"Great," said Lizzie. "I knew you'd mess it up."

"Me?" Charles asked. "It's your fault."

Scruffy sat on the floor between them, looking from one to the other like someone watching a Ping-Pong match. Then she lay down, put her chin on her paws, let out a big sigh, and gazed up at them with sad eyes. She wasn't smiling now.

Why are they always like this? I wish everyone could just be nice all the time.

"See what you did?" Lizzie asked. "You made Scruffy sad."

"No, you did!" Charles said.

"Charles, Lizzie!" called Dad from upstairs. "Bedtime, now."

They glared at each other one more time, then trudged up the stairs, too worn out from squabbling to even argue about whose turn it was with Scruffy. Scruffy followed them up and, without either of them noticing, turned into Mom and Dad's room. It was like she knew the only place to go for a peaceful sleep.

CHAPTER EIGHT

"I can't believe this is really happening," Lizzie said, leaning her head against the car window. She and Dad were on their way to Caring Paws, bringing Scruffy with them. She wasn't going to be the Petersons' foster puppy anymore. She was going to be put into a kennel, surrounded by a bunch of other dogs who needed homes. Scruffy was only just starting to get comfortable being around people, and now she was going to have to adjust to a whole new environment.

"It's not the end of the world," Dad said from the driver's seat.

"Hmph," Lizzie said, folding her arms across her chest.

"We'll still be able to see Scruffy, and you know there will be other foster puppies in our future, if—"

"I know, I know," said Lizzie. "If Charles and I can get along." She put a hand out to the mesh front of the puppy crate that was buckled in next to her, to say hi to Scruffy. Scruffy stretched her neck forward to sniff Lizzie's hand, then give her a tiny lick.

Thanks for being patient with me. I needed some extra time to get used to you!

Lizzie felt her throat close up, and tears sprang to her eyes. It wasn't that Caring Paws was a terrible place—it wasn't, at all. It was clean and bright, and Ms. Dobbins and her staff took great care of all the animals there. Scruffy would have a comfy bed, plenty of attention, and good food to eat. But it wasn't a home. It wasn't the home that Scruffy deserved.

Also, Scruffy was just getting over her shyness with people. Just that morning she had sat on Lizzie's lap and let herself be hugged.

But the worst part about the whole thing?

Lizzie knew that it was all her fault. Well, hers and Charles's, but as the older sister it was mostly her responsibility. How could she have let herself get into another argument with him? And how could they both have let Scruffy down like this?

"I wish Charles had come with us," she said now to Dad. "He was too upset. He couldn't stand to say good-bye to Scruffy."

"I know," Dad said. "To tell the truth, I was a little surprised that Mom felt the same way."

Lizzie managed a little smile. She knew what Dad meant. Mom was great with all their puppies, but she'd never really been a dog person. Still, now and then she fell in love with one of their fosters, and Scruffy had definitely found a place in her heart.

"On the bright side," Dad went on, meeting Lizzie's eyes in the rearview mirror, "Ms. Dobbins is pretty happy about all the publicity Scruffy will bring to Caring Paws. That means more animals will find good homes."

"I know," said Lizzie. "And when Rachel called to check in on Scruffy this morning she said she would tell Scruffy's followers where they can find Scruffy. Maybe someone will want to adopt her." Lizzie knew that Ms. Dobbins was as picky as the Petersons were about finding perfect homes for the pets in her care. People had to fill out a long application form and have an interview with Ms.

Dobbins or one of her staff people. Ms. Dobbins would never let Scruffy go home with just anyone.

Lizzie smiled down at Scruffy. "We'll find you the perfect home, don't worry," she said.

Scruffy tilted her head and smiled back at Lizzie.

I know you'll take good care of me.

"Whoa!" Dad said from the front seat as he pulled into the Caring Paws parking lot. The lot was full of cars, and there was a line of ten or fifteen people waiting to get inside the building. "What's this all about? Is there some special event here today?"

Lizzie laughed. "Nope," she said. "I have a feeling that all these people are here to see Scruffy." She knew how quickly news could travel on the Internet. If Rachel had posted something about Scruffy staying at Caring Paws, thousands of people would already have seen it.

Dad parked the car in one of the last empty spaces and pulled out his phone. "I'm just going to text Ms. Dobbins and let her know we're here," he said, poking at his phone. "Maybe someone can let us in the side door."

A few moments later his phone dinged. "Great," he said, reading Ms. Dobbins's reply. "She said she'll meet us there in a second."

He and Lizzie got out of the car, then Dad reached in for Scruffy's crate. "Let's try not to attract any attention," he said to Lizzie as he pulled it out. "I don't want people mobbing us. Scruffy wouldn't like that."

"Scruffy?" asked a young woman who was just passing by after getting out of her car. "Is that *the* Scruffy in there? Ooh, can I see? Can I get a selfie with her?"

Dad put his finger to his lips. "Easy," he said. "She's shy. Please let us get her settled inside. I'm sure everyone will get a chance to meet her."

The woman looked disappointed, but she nodded. "Okay," she said. Then she bent over to try to get a better look inside the crate. Dad cleared his throat, and the woman stood up and headed for a place on the line.

"Isn't it nuts?" Ms. Dobbins asked when she met them at the side door. "We're going to have to figure out some crowd control." She peeked into the crate. "Hello there, Ms. Superstar," she said. Then she waved them into a small, private room where people could spend time with pets they wanted to adopt. "Let's get her settled in here," she said. "This is going to be a long day for her—for all of us! In fact, I was thinking that maybe sleeping here in our kennel after all that might be a bit too much for Scruffy. Would you maybe be willing to have her stay with you overnight for a few nights, since she's already comfortable with your family?"

"Absolutely!" said Lizzie.

Dad put a hand on her shoulder. "Only if you and Charles can get along," he said. "And you'll have to make a schedule about whose room she sleeps in, so there's no arguing over that."

Lizzie nodded. "We'll get along," she promised. "I'll make sure of it." She was happy to know that she didn't have to say good-bye to Scruffy quite yet.

CHAPTER NINE

All that day, after Dad and Lizzie had brought Scruffy to Caring Paws, the house felt awfully quiet. Charles couldn't understand why; after all, it wasn't like tiny Scruffy was a noisy puppy. But for such a little thing she really did have a huge personality—and Charles was missing her. He missed her silly little ears, one up and one down. He missed her scraggly tail, and he missed her tiny paws. But most of all, he missed Scruffy's smile.

"I never saw a dog smile so much," he said to Lizzie as he passed her the measuring cup she'd asked for. Charles was helping Lizzie make a batch of her special homemade dog biscuits. They were Buddy's favorite. Really, all dogs loved them. Charles wasn't sure what Lizzie's secret ingredient was because she was always very mysterious about that. She'd let Charles pass her things, or wash up a bowl, or even sometimes measure out a teaspoon of this or a tablespoon of that. But she would never let him read her recipe, or be there for the whole process.

Lizzie didn't answer right away. She was checking the level of oil in the measuring cup he'd given her.

"I mean, I've seen a lot of dogs smile a little bit," Charles went on. "But never like Scruffy. She smiles all the time!" He watched as Lizzie poured the oil into a bowl, over a bunch of other ingredients, and started to mix.

"I know," she said as she stirred. "Maybe we can ask Mom to check Rachel's account. I miss that smile."

Charles pulled up a kitchen stool so he could watch Lizzie finish up the dough. He knew that baking treats was her way of keeping busy so that she didn't miss Scruffy so much. "At least she gets to sleep here tonight," he said. "You can have her in your room." He didn't want to get into an argument about it—it was so much nicer to be friends with his sister—so it was easier just to let her have the first turn with Scruffy. Anyway, the little pup had stayed with him the night before, so it really was Lizzie's turn.

"Aww, really?" Lizzie said. "I was going to say you could have her again. But I'd love that." Now she was rolling out the dough with a rolling pin.

Charles jumped up. "Can I help cut them out?" he asked. He loved using Lizzie's bone-shaped cookie cutters.

"Sure." Lizzie rolled a few more times, then stepped back, wiping her hands on her "I Love

Puppies" apron. "Go ahead," she said, handing Charles a cookie cutter.

Charles started stamping out cookies and placing them on baking sheets. As each one filled up, Lizzie carried it to the oven. Charles hoped they would decorate them later, too, with squiggles of delicious (to a dog) liver-flavored frosting.

"Now this is a happy scene," said Mom. She stood leaning in the doorway, smiling at them. "I love to see you two working together so nicely."

"Mom, can you find Rachel's special Scruffy account?" Lizzie asked.

Charles saw Mom roll her eyes. "You know I don't like social media," she said. "But—I know how much you two miss Scruffy. I miss her, too. It seems like forever until we're supposed to go pick her up." She pulled out her phone and tapped away, then peered at it and burst out laughing. "Oh, look at this," she said.

Charles and Lizzie crowded close so they could see. "Oh, yeah. That's the best smile ever!" said Charles.

"It looks like about twenty thousand people agree with you," Lizzie said. "Wow, Scruffy is more popular than ever!"

Just then, Mom's phone dinged with a text. She swiped to check it. "Oh! It's Ms. Dobbins. She wants us to come get Scruffy now!"

"What?" Lizzie asked. "I just put three trays of biscuits into the oven. Can't it wait?"

Mom shook her head. "I get the feeling they've had a rough day with so many people coming to see Scruffy." She picked the car keys off the hook by the door. "Dad's out in the backyard," she told Lizzie. "We'll be back soon."

"We?" Charles asked. "You mean I get to come?" He saw Lizzie's face freeze for a second, and knew she was envious. But then she smiled at him.

"You go," she said. "I'll have a welcome-home biscuit for her when you get back."

Charles bounced in his seat the whole way to Caring Paws. He couldn't wait to see Scruffy. When they arrived at the shelter, the parking lot was packed, just like Lizzie and Dad had said it was in the morning. And there was still a line of people waiting to see Scruffy, but Ms. Dobbins, who was guarding the door, waved Mom and Charles in.

"That's going to be it for today, folks," she said to the last of the crowd. "Come back tomorrow if you want to see Scruffy or any of the other wonderful pets we have available for loving homes."

People groaned, and Charles heard one guy yell, "Wait a second, you have to—" before the door closed behind them.

"Whew," said Ms. Dobbins. "What a crazy day! It's been nonstop. Everybody wants to meet

Scruffy." She led them to the quiet room in back, where Charles was surprised to see Rachel sitting on the floor with Scruffy in her lap. "Thank goodness for Rachel," Ms. Dobbins said. "We really don't have enough staff to cover a day like this, but she came right over when I called."

Scruffy looked up when Charles and Mom came into the room. She smiled at them, but then she curled back up into a ball and went to sleep.

"She's worn out, poor little thing," said Rachel, petting her. "We did our best to keep everything calm for her, but still—there were a lot of people in and out of this room, and everybody wanted a selfie."

"She must really like you," said Charles. "She doesn't sit in just anyone's lap."

"Rachel really gets Scruffy," Ms. Dobbins said, nodding. "Too bad she says she's not ready to adopt." She smiled at Mom and Charles. "But we'll find a home for Scruffy, for sure. Quite a few people filled out applications, and some even visited the other dogs, and our cat room."

"I think it's great that she's going home with you," Rachel said to Mom and Charles. "I'm sure she feels safe and secure at your house."

"Exactly," said Ms. Dobbins. "I imagine the crowd has disappeared by now, so you can just take her right out the front door."

Rachel and Charles helped Scruffy get comfortable in the puppy crate. The little pup could barely keep her eyes open, but she licked Charles's hand and wagged her scraggly tail.

Can we go home now?

Mom picked up the crate and they all headed for the door. As Ms. Dobbins pushed it open for them, Charles heard that guy yelling again. "You have to let me see that puppy. I think she's mine!"

CHAPTER TEN

Charles stared at the man, then looked back at Ms. Dobbins. She stood calmly with her arms crossed. "Well," she said. "If that's the case, of course you should certainly have a chance to see Scruffy. Let's all go inside quietly so we don't upset her, though."

She opened the door so the man could come in, and led the way back to the quiet room. Rachel followed her, and so did Charles, with Mom bringing up the rear carrying Scruffy's crate.

Charles's heart was pounding. Was this yelling man really Scruffy's true owner? How was he going to feel if the shy little puppy had to go home with this man? Hopefully, he was a nice guy; maybe he was just a little upset over having to wait so long to see the puppy he thought belonged to him.

"I wish you had called us to talk about this," Ms. Dobbins said to the man. "We would have made sure you had a chance to see Scruffy sooner instead of waiting on line with everyone else."

"I didn't think of it," he said. "Well? Can I see her?"

"You can," said Ms. Dobbins. "But you can't touch her. She's just getting used to people, and right now Rachel is the only one who she totally trusts."

Ms. Dobbins nodded to Mom, who put the crate down and opened the door. Rachel bent down to help Scruffy out and held her securely in her arms.

The man stepped forward and peered at Scruffy. The puppy dipped her head down and smiled up at him. This time, Charles could really see how Scruffy's smile might mean that she was frightened. He could tell that she wasn't sure at all about this person. Charles held his breath and crossed his fingers. He really did not want this man to be Scruffy's owner.

Then the man stepped back. "Nope," he said. "My dog was much bigger than this one. I couldn't really tell from the pictures, but this isn't my puppy. Guess I have to just keep looking for Maybelle."

Charles almost let out a wild giggle. *Maybelle?* Instead, he let out a quiet sigh of relief as Rachel tucked Scruffy back into the crate. He gave Mom a *Can we go now?* look, and she nodded. Once again, they all paraded back to the door. They stood watching as the man got into his car.

Ms. Dobbins waved him off. "I suppose I should have encouraged him to look at some of our other pets available for adoption," she said, "but I didn't have a great feeling about him." She shrugged and smiled at Charles. "Have a nice evening with Scruffy," she said. "I expect another busy day tomorrow, so I'm glad she can rest up with you."

Lizzie jumped up when she heard Mom's car in the driveway. "They're here!" she called to Dad. She couldn't wait to see Scruffy again. She and Buddy ran to the door to welcome the smiley puppy home.

"Rachel!" said Lizzie when she saw the vet tech climbing out of the car.

"We made her come home with us, for dinner," Mom said, smiling at Rachel. "Scruffy's gotten kind of used to having her around."

"You should have seen what just happened at Caring Paws," Charles said as they came inside, Rachel carrying Scruffy's crate. He launched into the story, telling Lizzie about the man who thought Scruffy might be his.

"Oh, no," said Lizzie. She bent to open up Scruffy's crate. "Hey, cutie," she said as Scruffy smiled up at her.

I sure didn't want to go home with that guy. I feel so much more comfortable with you people.

"She did great today," said Rachel. She sat down on the floor and let Scruffy come to her. "It wasn't easy for her, being the center of attention. I can relate to that!"

"Ms. Dobbins said that you made her feel comfortable all day," Mom said to Rachel. "I think Scruffy really trusts you. Maybe it's because you were one of the first people to help her, at Dr. Gibson's office."

"I think it's more than that," said Lizzie, watching Scruffy as the little pup climbed right into Rachel's lap. "I think Scruffy knows that the two of you are meant to be together."

Rachel looked up at Lizzie, surprised. "Really?

You think so? But I already told Ms. Dobbins I'm not ready to adopt a dog. I mean, we had dogs when I was a kid, but I've never had one all on my own."

"Tell me this," said Lizzie. "How did you feel when you thought that guy might take Scruffy away forever?"

Rachel's eyes widened and she put a hand over her mouth. "Awful," she whispered. "I felt awful."

Lizzie nodded. "You might not be ready, but Scruffy sure is," she said.

"Lizzie's right," Charles said. "Scruffy loves you. It's obvious."

Rachel buried her nose in Scruffy's fur. When she looked up again, her eyes were teary. "I love her, too," she said. "What am I waiting for? I guess I was wrong. I am ready for a dog of my very own—as long as it's this dog."

Scruffy wagged her scraggly tail and licked Rachel's face.

We're going to be very happy together! I can already tell.

"Well, that makes two things to celebrate tonight," said Mom.

"Um, number one is that Scruffy has found the perfect home. What's the other thing?" Lizzie asked.

"I haven't heard you and Charles argue all day," Mom said. "And I have a feeling your bickering phase might be over, now that you've remembered how much nicer it is to get along."

Lizzie and Charles smiled at each other. At the exact same moment, they both held up their pinkies. Linking them, they chanted, "Best buds, a—ooo—gah!"

Everybody cracked up, and Scruffy gave them one of her biggest grins ever. Charles and Lizzie smiled at each other. It was good to be best buds again.

PUPPY TIPS

Have you ever met a stray dog like Scruffy? If you see a stray dog, it's probably best to get a grown-up before you try to help. A dog who has been living on its own can be frightened, shy, and not used to people. Lizzie and Charles did the right thing when they asked their dad for help getting Scruffy unstuck.

Dear Reader,

I got the idea to write about a smiling dog because my dog, Zipper, is a big smiler. I think it started with him trying to show that he wasn't a threat—but he gets such a happy reaction when he does it that he started to smile more and more. Some new people still wonder if he's snarling at them, but I'm always quick to let them know that he's smiling. Zipper is the sweetest guy around and I've never even heard him growl at anyone; he wouldn't hurt a fly. I've tried to get pictures of Zipper smiling, but the smiles come and go so quickly that it's very hard. Does your dog smile?

Yours from the Puppy Place,

Ellen Miles

For another book about a
big furry sweetheart, try KODIAK or LUCKY.